The Berenstain Bears'
NEW NEIGHBORS

Uh-oh. Some nearby neighbors
moved away.
<u>Now</u> who's coming here
to stay?

A FIRST TIME BOOK®

The Berenstain Bears'
NEW NEIGHBORS

Stan & Jan Berenstain

Random House New York

Copyright © 1994 by Berenstain Enterprises, Inc. All rights reserved
under International and Pan-American Copyright Conventions. Published
in the United States by Random House, Inc., New York, and simultaneously
in Canada by Random House of Canada Limited, Toronto.

Library of Congress Cataloging-in-Publication Data
Berenstain, Stan   The Berenstain Bears' new neighbor / by Stan and Jan
Berenstain.   p.   cm. — (First time books)   SUMMARY: Papa Bear learns
a lesson in the importance of acceptance when a new family of pandas
moves in across the road.
ISBN: 0-679-86435-0 (pbk.) — 0-679-96435-5 (lib. bdg.)
[1. Bears—Fiction.   2. Pandas—Fiction.   3. Neighborliness—Fiction.
4. Prejudices—Fiction.]   I. Berenstain, Jan.   II. Title.   III. Series: Berenstain,
Stan. First time books.   PZ7.B4483Bfb   1994   [E]—dc20 . 93-47145

Manufactured in the United States of America   65 64 63

"I wonder how long it will be empty," said Sister Bear. She was talking about the house across the road. The family that had lived there had moved to Big Bear City. Now the house was empty and had a "for sale" sign on it.

"It's hard to say," said Papa Bear.

"I don't think it will be empty very long," said Mama. "It's a very nice house."

"I just hope whoever moves in has cubs," said Brother Bear.

"Especially girls," said Sister. Just then, Mrs. McBear, the real-estate person, drove up and stopped in front of the empty house.

FOR SALE

She got out of her car
and hammered a "sold" sign
over the "for sale" sign.

"How about that?" said Papa. "Somebody bought it already." He called across the road, "Say, Mrs. McBear! Who'll be moving in?"

"Hi, Bear family!" she said. "Can't talk right now! Too busy!" Then she got into her car, waved, and drove away.

"Hmm," said Papa. "That's not like Mrs. McBear. She usually has plenty to say."

"Maybe she doesn't *know* who'll be moving in," suggested Mama.

"Of course she knows," said Papa. "Whoever it is, she sold them the house, didn't she?"

"I suppose so," said Mama. "But I don't know what difference it makes."

"It makes a lot of difference," said Papa. "It's important who your neighbors are."

"I just hope whoever moves in has cubs," said Brother.

"Especially girls," said Sister.

Over the next few days, the Bears went about their business. Papa worked in his wood shop.

Mama had a lot of tulip bulbs she wanted to put in.

Brother and Sister went to school in the morning and came home in the afternoon.

Once in a while, they wondered what their new neighbors would be like. Would they be young or old? Would they be friendly, or would they keep to themselves?

"Hey," said Brother early one morning. "Our new neighbors are moving in. And they *do* have cubs." Sister ran to the window.

"Any girls?" she said.

"Yep," said Brother. "Two girls and one boy—and look, the boy is into sports. At least, he's kicking a soccer ball around. Come on, Sis. Let's go over and play."

"Now hold on, please," said Mama, who had joined the cubs at the window.

"But, Mama," said Sister, "it's Saturday, and we don't have to go to school."

"We've got to give them a chance to get moved in," Mama said. "They do look like a lovely family. We'll all go over later and welcome them."

"Hmm," said Papa, looking out of the window. "Now, who do you suppose they are," he added in a grumpy tone of voice, "and what do you suppose they're doing here?"

"Well," said Mama. "I suppose they're the Panda family, because that's what they've just painted on their mailbox. As for what they're doing, I suppose they're doing the same thing we are—living here."

"What's the matter, Papa?" asked Sister. "Don't you like them?"

"That's not it," he said. "It's just. It's just that they're... *different*, that's all."

"Well, different or not," said Mama as they sat down for breakfast, "they're our new neighbors, and later today we're going to welcome them with a jar of our special honey."

"Besides," she continued, "I thought you *liked* things to be different. When we were at the bulb farm, you complained when I wanted to buy all yellow tulips. 'Get *different* colors,' you said. The cubs agreed with you. So I got yellow, red, and blue." Papa didn't say anything. He just kept eating and looking grumpy. "And you always use different kinds of wood in your furniture work," she went on. "And if we have the same thing for dinner three nights in a row, you say, 'Not the same thing again! Why can't we have something different?'"

"That's different," grumped Papa as he left the breakfast table. "Just look at that, would you?" he said, looking out the window.

"Before you start giving away all of our special honey, I think you should have a look at what our new neighbors are doing. They've hardly even moved in, and they're building a fence— a spite fence."

"What's a spite fence, Papa?" asked Sister.
Mama looked out the window and saw that
the Pandas did seem to be putting up
some sort of fence. Though it didn't
look like any fence she'd ever seen.
It looked more like a row of sticks.

"A spite fence," said Papa, "is a
fence that bad neighbors put up
just for spite. They do it just to be
mean and keep decent folks from
seeing what they're up to."

"I'm sure there's an explanation," Mama said. She was back in the kitchen putting a big red bow on a jar of special honey.

"Humpf," said Papa. "I was saving that honey for a special occasion."

"New neighbors *are* a special occasion," she said.

"Hi, neighbors!" said Brother. "We're Brother and Sister Bear!" He and Sister had decided not to wait for the family welcoming visit. "We live in that big tree house across the road."

"I'm Peter Panda," said the new cub. "These are my sisters, Pam and Patty." The new cubs were very friendly, and pretty soon one and all were busy talking about the things cubs talk about.

It turned out that Peter Panda not only had a soccer ball, he was a soccer whiz. But he didn't know much about baseball or football. He agreed to show Brother some soccer moves if Brother would teach him about baseball and football.

Sister, Pam, and Patty were already
working up a sweat jumping rope.

And it turned out that the "spite fence" wasn't even a fence. It was a row of bamboo. "It's our favorite food," explained Peter. "Mom is a great bamboo cook. She must have fifty recipes."

"Our favorite food is honey," said Brother. "We're going to bring you a jar of it later."

That afternoon the whole Bear family came over to welcome their new neighbors with a jar of special honey. The Bears and the Pandas had a very pleasant visit. Even Papa had a good time.

He found Mr. Panda, who had traveled all over the world, to be a very interesting fellow. And he especially enjoyed the chilled bamboo juice that Mr. Panda served.

Mama arranged a neighborhood welcome
at the community center for the next weekend.
It was a covered-dish supper, and Mrs. Panda's
barbecued bamboo shoots were the hit of the
evening.